The C...
WINTER

By Danna Smith
Illustrated by Amber Ren

A GOLDEN BOOK • NEW YORK

Text copyright © 2019 by Danna Smith.
Cover art and interior illustrations copyright © 2019 by Amber Ren.
All rights reserved. Published in the United States by Golden Books, an imprint of Random House
Children's Books, a division of Penguin Random House LLC, 1745 Broadway, New York, NY 10019.
Golden Books, A Golden Book, A Little Golden Book, the G colophon,
and the distinctive gold spine are registered trademarks
of Penguin Random House LLC.
rhcbooks.com
Educators and librarians, for a variety of teaching tools, visit us at
RHTeachersLibrarians.com
Library of Congress Control Number: 2017944973
ISBN 978-1-5247-6892-8 (trade) — ISBN 978-1-5247-6893-5 (ebook)
Printed in the United States of America
10 9 8 7 6 5 4 3 2 1

WHITE is out the window.
Look at all the snow!

RED is Grandma's old sled.
Up the hill we go.

SILVER are the shiny blades
speeding to the end.

YELLOW is an old scarf
we share with our new friend.

BLACK are all the wild birds
singing in the tree.

GRAY are little footprints
that like to follow me.

PINK are my rosy cheeks,
cold from winter fun.

ORANGE is a soft goodbye from the setting sun.

TAN is my sleepy dog,
who jumps on for a ride.

GREEN are my soggy boots.
I leave them both outside.

TURQUOISE is the handle of my favorite cup.

BROWN is the cocoa
that warms my insides up.

BLUE are my slippers,
which cover chilly feet.

PURPLE is my Grandma's lap—
the softest, warmest seat.